Sherlock Holmes and The Unwanted Client

Mabel Swift

Sherlock Holmes and The Unwanted Client

(A Sherlock Holmes Mystery - Book 8)

By

Mabel Swift

Copyright 2024 by Mabel Swift

www.mabelswift.com

This is a work of fiction and any resemblance to any person living or dead is purely coincidental.

Contents

Chapter 1

The rain had ceased its relentless assault on Baker Street, leaving behind a damp chill that seeped through the windows of 221B. Sherlock Holmes stood by the fireplace, his tall, lean figure silhouetted against the flickering flames. He prodded the embers with a poker, coaxing them back to life. Dr John Watson sat in his customary armchair, a new mystery novel open on his lap, though his tired eyes had long since ceased their perusal of the text.

The clock on the mantelpiece chimed the hour, its sonorous tones echoing through the room.

Holmes turned from the fire, his grey eyes scanning the cluttered space with a restless energy.

"I fear, Watson, that we are in for a quiet day. The criminal classes seem to have taken a holiday."

Watson chuckled as he closed his book. "Perhaps they've been deterred by the weather. Even the most determined villain might think twice about venturing out in this damp."

Before Holmes could reply, there came a gentle knock at the door.

Mrs Hudson, their landlady, entered. "There's a gentleman to see you. A Mr Knight."

Holmes said, "Show him in, Mrs Hudson."

The landlady nodded and hurried from the room. A moment later, she ushered in a man who appeared to be in his late twenties. He was dressed in a manner that spoke of modest means but with careful attention to his appearance. His dark hair was neatly combed, and his moustache was trimmed with precision. He carried himself with an air of quiet confidence, though Holmes didn't miss the flicker of unease in his blue eyes.

"Mr Holmes, Dr Watson," the man said, nodding to each in turn. "I'm Toby Knight. I hope I'm not intruding."

Holmes took a seat and gestured to the chair opposite Watson. "Not at all, Mr Knight. Please, be seated and tell us what brings you here on this dreary afternoon."

Knight settled into the chair. "It's a delicate matter, Mr Holmes. I find myself in need of your unique talents."

Watson asked, "How may we be of assistance, Mr Knight?"

Knight drew a deep breath as if steeling himself. "I'm a fortune teller by trade. And I–"

Before he could continue, Holmes leapt to his feet, his face contorted with sudden anger. The detective's grey eyes flashed with a cold fury that Watson had rarely witnessed.

"A fortune teller?" Holmes spat the words as if they left a foul taste in his mouth. "I will never have a fortune teller as a client, Mr Knight. Never!"

Knight recoiled, startled by the vehemence of Holmes's reaction. "But Mr Holmes, I–"

Holmes cut him off with a sharp gesture. "It's no secret that I despise your kind, Mr Knight. Fortune tellers, mediums, spiritualists, and so on. You're all cut from the same cloth. Charlatans and frauds, preying on the grief and gullibility of others. You take advantage of people at their most vulnerable, offering false hope and empty promises."

Watson rose, placing a calming hand on his friend's arm. "Holmes, perhaps we should hear Mr Knight out."

But Holmes shook off Watson's hand, his voice rising. "No, Watson. I will not be party to this man's deceptions. I have dedicated my life to the pursuit of truth and logic. I will not sully my reputation by associating with one who makes his living through trickery and lies."

Knight stood, his face pale but his voice steady. "Mr Holmes, I assure you, I am not here to deceive you. My situation is–"

"Your situation, Mr Knight, is of no interest to me," Holmes interrupted, his tone cold and final. "I suggest you take your unwanted problem elsewhere. There are plenty of gullible fools in London who will gladly listen to whatever problem plagues you. I, however, am not one of them."

Watson watched the exchange with growing concern. He had seen Holmes dismiss potential clients before, but never with such unbridled contempt. He said, "Holmes, surely we can at least listen to what Mr Knight has to say."

Holmes faced his friend. "No, Watson. I will not compromise my principles, not even for you. Mr Knight and his ilk represent everything I stand against. I will not give him a moment more of my time."

Turning back to Knight, who stood frozen in shock, Holmes pointed towards the door. "Leave, Mr Knight. Take your unwanted problem and your dubious profession elsewhere. You'll find no help here."

Knight's shoulders slumped in defeat. He reached for his hat, which he had placed on a nearby table. "I'm sorry to have troubled you, Mr Holmes. I had hoped... but never mind. Good day to you both."

As Knight moved towards the door, Watson felt a pang of sympathy for the man. Whatever his profession, he had clearly come to them in genuine distress. The doctor's compassionate nature warred with his loyalty to Holmes, but in the end, his innate kindness won out.

"Mr Knight," Watson said. "Perhaps you could tell us what your problem is. We might be able to offer a little advice, at least."

Holmes held his hand up. "Watson, I will have no part in this charade. If you insist on entertaining this charlatan, you may do so without me."

With that, Holmes stormed out of the room, slamming the door behind him with enough force to rattle the windows. Watson winced at the sound but gestured for Knight to retake his seat.

The fortune teller sank back into the chair and gave the good doctor a small smile. "Thank you, Dr Watson. I appreciate your time. I'm not sure where to begin with my problem."

Watson settled into his own chair. "Start at the beginning, Mr Knight. What's troubling you?"

Knight answered, "It's my predictions; the ones I give to my clients. They're coming true, but not in the way they should."

Watson's brow furrowed. "I'm not sure I understand. Isn't that what your clients want? For your predictions to come true?"

Knight shook his head. "No, no. You see, when I make a prediction, it's meant to be positive. A glimpse of a bright future. But lately, these predictions have been turning into something unfortunate, and three of my clients have suffered as a result. Over the last few weeks, they have complained to me about what's happened to them and claimed it was all my fault. I could only apologise to them. But these complaints have become known somehow, and now they are affecting my business and my reputation. There are rumours circulating that I've been cursing my clients and wishing them bad luck."

"Cursing them?" Watson said. "But surely people don't believe that?"

"They do," Knight said. "And I don't know what to do. I've built my business on trust, on giving people hope. But now? Now, they look at me with fear, with suspicion. And I don't know what to do about this matter."

Watson's concern deepened. While he shared Holmes' scepticism about fortune telling, he couldn't ignore the genuine distress radiating from the man before him. "Mr Knight, have you considered that these unfortunate events might be coincidences? Perhaps exaggerated by your clients?"

"I've considered that, of course. But the predictions have all turned sour within the last two weeks. This can't be a coincidence. I fear someone is targeting my clients with a view to sabotaging my business."

"Sabotage? Do you have any evidence to support this?"

Knight replied, "No, I don't, but I think it's the only explanation. I have a growing sense of dread. I wonder how far this person will go to sabotage my business. I worry that some of my clients may even come to physical harm. I couldn't live with myself if that happened."

"Mr Knight," Watson said, choosing his words with care. "I understand your concerns, and I can see why you sought out Mr Holmes' assistance. However, without concrete evidence, it may be difficult to pursue this matter further."

Knight sighed. "I understand. I didn't know where else to turn. The police would laugh me out of the station if I went to them with this."

Watson felt a twinge of guilt at the man's dejected tone. Despite Holmes' objections, he couldn't simply turn Knight away without offering some form of help.

"Perhaps," Watson said, "you could provide me with more details about these incidents. While I can't promise anything, I might be able to offer some advice or see if there's a pattern somewhere."

Knight's eyes lit up with a glimmer of hope. "You'd do that, Dr Watson? Even after Mr Holmes' reaction?"

Watson smiled wryly. "Mr Holmes and I don't always see eye to eye on every matter. And while I share his scepticism about certain practices, I can't ignore a cry for help. Now, tell me more about these predictions and their unfortunate outcomes."

Before Knight could speak, the door was flung open.

Chapter 2

Holmes strode back into the room and announced, "I must confess that I overheard your conversation."

Watson's eyebrows rose slightly, and he suspected that Holmes had been listening at the door. However, he wisely kept this thought to himself.

Holmes continued, his tone softening slightly, "Mr Knight, while I maintain my stance on the dubious nature of fortune-telling, I cannot overlook the potential risk to public safety. It is my duty to protect the innocent, regardless of the circumstances that bring such matters to my attention."

Knight nodded and didn't say a word.

"Moreover," Holmes added, "I find myself rather curious about the peculiar nature of these events. Mr Knight, if you would be so kind as to continue your tale, I believe we may uncover something of interest."

Knight said, "Thank you, Mr Holmes. Before I proceed, I must confess something. I also share your views on fortune-tellers and mediums. Or at least, I did once."

Holmes settled into his armchair. "Indeed? Do elaborate."

Knight continued, "Before I undertook my present career, I used to work behind the scenes at The Royal Crescent Theatre. Set design, prop management, that sort of thing. It was there that I first encountered the world of mediums and psychics. I was fascinated by their shows, and as I watched from the sidelines, I worked out how they did it. How they would pick up on little details about a person's appearance or manner of speaking. And, of course, the things people would say gave the performers a lot of information. The medium or psychic would listen and then make vague predictions which could easily apply to that person. Having seen how they worked, I saw how the performers tricked people into believing whatever they said. It was all an act; I had no doubt about that."

Holmes asked, "So how did you go from sceptic to practitioner?"

Knight chuckled ruefully. "It was a bet between me and a friend of mine, Harry Matthews, who works as a carpenter at the theatre. One night, we were in the wings watching a particularly popular medium on stage. I told Harry I could do the same thing, that it was all about observation and clever wordplay. He didn't believe me, so we made a wager."

"And you won, I take it?" Watson asked.

Knight nodded. "At first, it was just a lark. I set up a small booth at a local fair. I read palms and used tarot cards. It was fun and I enjoyed talking to people. I gave them vague predictions, based on what they'd revealed to me, like I'd seen with the mediums on stage. But then something strange happened. People started coming back, telling me how accurate my readings had been."

Watson said, "Coincidence, surely?"

"That's what I thought at first," Knight admitted. "But as time went on, my reputation grew. I found myself able to make more specific predictions, ones that seemed to come true with alarming regularity."

"How do you explain this accuracy?" Watson asked.

Knight shrugged. "I can't. Perhaps I've developed some sort of intuition, or maybe I'm just very good at reading people. But the fact remains, my words began to carry weight. And as my reputation grew, I found myself in need of a more permanent location for my business. My lodgings seemed the most logical choice, so I approached my landlord with the proposition. The fellow was sceptical at first, but he agreed to allow me to use the front room for my readings, but with one condition. He wanted a cut of my takings."

Watson tutted. "That seems rather opportunistic of him."

Knight said, "Perhaps, but I was making enough money that I could afford to be generous. Besides, it allowed me to leave my position at the theatre and focus on my new career full-time."

Holmes said, "Mr Knight, I see from your wedding band that you are married. May I ask, how did your wife react to this change in circumstances?"

A fond smile softened Knight's features. "I met Ava, my wife, at The Royal Crescent Theatre, three years ago. She was working as a seamstress at the time. When I told her about my fortune-telling plans, she was supportive from the start. She's always been my biggest champion. In fact, she was so enthusiastic about the venture that she left her job at the theatre to become my assistant."

"Assistant?" Watson queried.

Knight nodded. "Yes, she manages the practical side of things, like greeting clients, showing them into the reading room, that sort of thing. She's also very good at comforting clients who may have become over-emotional after one of their readings. But emotional in a good way, you understand. Clients often reveal their vulnerable side to me, which leads to an outpouring of feelings, which can be cathartic for them."

Watson said, "It sounds as though you've built quite a successful enterprise. Please, tell us more about those predictions that have taken a troubling turn."

Knight began, "There have been three clients who have complained to me. The first was Miss Gwendolyn Fairchild, a young woman who works in a textile factory. She came to me, seeking advice about her prospects for marriage. I told her to remain positive and open to any possibility of suitors, even those she wouldn't normally consider. She was happy to accept my suggestions."

Holmes nodded. "And the outcome?"

Knight continued, "Miss Fairchild took my advice to heart. She began courting a charming man, someone she admitted she wouldn't have given a second glance before. Their romance quickly flourished, and they fell in love. But then..." He trailed off, shaking his head.

"But then?" Watson prompted gently.

"The man turned out to be a scoundrel," Knight said. "He stole from her, leaving her in severe financial difficulties. She blames me for encouraging her to be open to someone she wouldn't normally consider."

"I see," Holmes said. "And the second client?"

Knight replied, "Mr Cyril Thorne, a struggling journalist. He came to me seeking advice on how to succeed in his work. I advised him to widen his circle of contacts and not to be afraid of digging deeper into stories, to push beyond his usual safety zone."

"A reasonable suggestion for a journalist," Watson remarked.

"Yes," Knight agreed. "But the results were disastrous. Following my advice, Mr Thorne ventured into the seedier parts of the city. He met an informer who passed him secrets about a certain politician, claiming to have proof of his wrongdoing. Thorne published the story, but it turned out to be false, as was the evidence he'd been given. He was sacked from his position and now blames me for the advice that led him down the wrong path."

"And the third client?" Holmes asked.

Knight sighed heavily. "Mr Leonard Endicott, a prominent investment banker. He sought insight into his financial ventures, asking if he should take more risks. I advised him to be cautious but to always trust his instincts. Shortly after our consultation, Endicott decided against a new investment opportunity. However, his colleagues went ahead with it and made a fortune. Now, he holds me responsible for his missed opportunity."

A heavy silence fell over the room as Holmes and Watson absorbed the information.

After a moment, Holmes spoke, "Mr Knight, my initial thoughts were that these clients of yours had run into a bit of bad luck, as happens with many people, and they decided to place the blame on you. But there is something bothering me about these stories. I sense there is a link somewhere, and I'd like to dig deeper into that possibility. There could be foul play at work here. Tell me, in your professional capacity, have you made any enemies? Perhaps a rival fortune-teller or medium who might resent your success?"

"I suppose it's possible," Knight said. "But I've never made contact with people who have a similar occupation to mine, apart from those I came across during my work at the theatre. Do you think a rival could be behind these issues, Mr Holmes?"

"As you said, it could be a possibility. Someone may resent your success and wants to see you fail." He gave Knight a long, studious look. The poor man shifted under the detective's scrutiny. Holmes said, "Despite the nature of your work, this situation has captured my curiosity. Very well, Mr Knight. We shall look into this matter. Could you provide us with the details of the clients you mentioned? Any information you have on Miss Fairchild, Mr Thorne, and Mr Endicott would be most helpful."

Knight sat up straighter, the relief evident on his face. "Of course, Mr Holmes. I'll give you what I can, though I'm afraid it's rather limited." He proceeded to give details of where his clients worked, or had worked, in the case of the dismissed journalist.

Watson wrote the details down in his notebook. He said, "And their addresses?"

"I'm afraid I don't have their home addresses," Knight replied. "I only know their work details because it came up during my readings with them."

Holmes said, "No matter. We shall make do with what we have. Now, Mr Knight, we'll need your address as well. Where might we find you should we require further information?"

Knight replied, "Ah, yes. I've recently moved into larger lodgings to accommodate my growing business. You can find me at Clarence Gardens, just off Regent's Park." He gave the number of the house.

Holmes stood abruptly, signalling the end of the interview. "Thank you, Mr Knight. Dr Watson and I will look into these matters and contact you in due course."

Knight rose as well. "Thank you, Mr Holmes, Dr Watson. I can't express how grateful I am for your assistance."

As Watson showed Knight to the door, Holmes paced the room, his mind already piecing together the puzzle before him. Once the door closed behind their client, Holmes turned to his friend.

"Well, Watson, what do you make of this new case?"

Watson returned to his seat, stroking his moustache thoughtfully. "It's a curious case, Holmes. On the surface, it seems like a string of unfortunate coincidences. But given your aversion to such explanations, I suspect there's more to it."

Holmes nodded. "Indeed, Watson. The question is, are we dealing with a case of sabotage or is there something else at play? Perhaps our fortune-teller is not as innocent as he appears."

"You suspect Knight himself?" Watson asked.

"I do," Holmes replied. "Knight's story of transitioning from a sceptic to a successful fortune-teller is intriguing, to say the least. And we must take into account that deception is the foundation of his business. I suggest we start with The Royal Crescent Theatre. I would like to speak to his former colleague, Mr Matthews, and find out more about Mr Knight's character and the circumstances of his departure."

"Agreed," Watson said, rising from his chair. "Shall we head there now?"

Holmes nodded his assent, a glimmer of excitement dancing in his eyes. With a swift, practised motion, he reached for his hat, perched on its usual hook by the door. As he settled it atop his head, adjusting the brim just so, Watson could sense the familiar thrill of the chase beginning to course through his friend's veins. The game, as Holmes was fond of saying, was most decidedly afoot.

Chapter 3

A while later, the carriage carrying Holmes and Watson rattled to a stop outside The Royal Crescent Theatre, its wheels clattering against the uneven cobblestones. Holmes alighted first and then offered a hand to Watson.

As they approached the entrance, a stagehand, his face smeared with dirt and sweat, hurried out of a side door, carrying an armful of props.

"Pardon me," Holmes called out. "We're looking for Harry Matthews. Might you know where we can find him?"

The stagehand paused, shifting his load. "Matthews? Aye, he'll be backstage, working on the new set. Head through that side door there, can't miss him."

Holmes nodded his thanks, and the pair made their way to the indicated entrance. The door creaked open, revealing a dimly lit corridor. They navigated the narrow passage, ducking under low-hanging ropes and sidestepping piles of discarded props.

The backstage area was a hive of activity. Stagehands scurried about, carrying pieces of scenery and props. Actors in various states of dress rehearsed their lines in hushed tones. Amidst the chaos, they spotted a man working on an ornate wooden staircase that led to nowhere.

"Mr Matthews?" Holmes inquired, approaching the man.

The carpenter looked up, his face breaking into a friendly smile. "That's me. What can I do for you gentlemen?"

"I'm Sherlock Holmes, and this is my colleague, Dr Watson. We'd like to ask you a few questions about Mr Toby Knight."

Matthews' eyes lit up with recognition. "Toby? A great chap, he is. What would you like to know about him?"

"What can you tell me about his character?" Holmes asked.

Matthews replied, "Toby always had a bit of mischief about him, but he was a hard worker nonetheless. We worked side by side for years. He helped me with the set pieces. He had a keen eye for detail when it came to woodwork. As well as helping me, Toby turned his hand to whatever needed doing backstage. Never one to shy away from hard work."

Holmes said, "We've heard about a certain bet between you two. Regarding his, shall we say, career change?"

A hearty laugh escaped from Matthews. "Oh, that! I thought he'd gone mad when he first mentioned it. Becoming a fortune-teller, of all things! I told him he was daft, but he was determined to prove me wrong."

"And the terms of this bet?" Holmes asked.

Matthews shook his head, still chuckling. "It was nothing extravagant, mind you. Just a pint and a meal at the local pub. I was certain Toby was going to lose the bet, so I made sure the wager was within his budget. I didn't want to fleece the poor lad when he lost the wager. Shows what I know, eh? But I was happy to settle the wager and treated us to a couple of pints and a great meal."

Watson scribbled in his notebook and then asked, "So, you were surprised by his success?"

"Surprised? You can say that again!" Matthews exclaimed. "Never thought he'd make a go of it, but here we are. Last I heard, he's doing quite well for himself. Good for him, I say."

Holmes' expression grew serious. "Mr Matthews, we've been informed there have been some issues with Mr

Knight's predictions as of late. Some are coming true but in rather unfortunate ways."

The smile faded from Matthews' face, replaced by a look of concern. "What do you mean? Is Toby alright?"

"He's fine," Watson reassured him quickly. "But we're trying to determine if someone might be interfering with his work."

"Interfering? I can't imagine who'd want to do that. Toby's a good sort, never had an enemy during his time here."

Holmes asked, "Mr Matthews, can you think of anyone who might have a reason to sabotage Mr Knight's business?"

Matthews ran a hand through his hair causing a light shower of sawdust to flutter down to the floor. "Well," he began hesitantly, "I hate to speak ill of anyone, especially her, but there might be one person."

Holmes said, "Please, do go on."

Matthews said, "Ava. Toby's wife. Don't get me wrong, she's a lovely woman, and I'm quite fond of her. But she's always had a jealous streak."

Watson's pen paused over his notebook. "You think she might be behind this?"

"I don't know for certain," Matthews admitted. "But the audience who attend psychic shows here are mainly women. I assume Toby's work might involve visits from many women, too. Ava might not take kindly to that."

Holmes nodded thoughtfully. "An interesting theory. But how do you suppose she could be sabotaging his predictions?"

Matthews shrugged helplessly. "I've no idea. It's just a thought, mind you. I could be way off the mark."

"Every piece of information is valuable," Holmes assured him. "One last question, if I may. Where might we find Mrs Knight at this hour?"

Matthews scratched his chin thoughtfully. "She's likely at home. They've got a place near Regent's Park now, I believe. Quite a step up from their old lodgings, I can tell you."

"Thank you, Mr Matthews," Holmes said, extending his hand. "You've been most helpful."

As they turned to leave, Matthews called after them, "I do hope Toby's alright. He deserves to be successful. He's a good man."

Chapter 4

Sometime later, Holmes and Watson stepped out of the hansom cab onto the well-kept street near Regent's Park. They approached a house with a freshly painted green door and a polished brass knocker. Watson reached out and rapped three times. The sound echoed in the quiet street.

After a moment, light footsteps could be heard approaching from within. The door swung open, revealing a woman in her late twenties, her auburn hair neatly pinned back and her dress simple but well-made.

"Mr Holmes, Dr Watson," she said, a smile spreading across her face. "Toby said you might pay me a call, but he didn't say why. He said it was something to do with a few clients of his, something that was causing him concern. He said it was nothing for me to worry about but to speak to you if you turn up. Oh, goodness me! I can't stand here chatting with you on the doorstep. Please, do come in.

You've arrived at a fortunate time as I've just made a fresh pot of tea."

As they stepped into the narrow hallway, the scent of beeswax polish and lavender filled the air. Ava Knight led them into a large sitting room, gesturing for them to take a seat on the floral-patterned sofa.

She asked how they took their tea, and then poured the hot, amber liquid into delicate cups which she passed to them. She sat down, her hands crossed on her lap, a soft smile on her face.

Mrs Knight said, "I know Toby is trying to protect me from whatever is troubling him, but can you tell me if my husband is okay? That he's not in danger, or anything like that. It would help to settle my mind, but I completely understand if you're not at liberty to tell me."

"I can confirm your husband is fine, and as far as I'm aware, he is not in danger," Holmes said. "I am certain that Dr Watson and I will successfully assist him in solving the issue that troubles your husband. We do require background information to do that, hence our visit to you. Mrs Knight, we'd like to hear more about your husband's business. How did it all begin?"

Mrs Knight's eyes sparkled with amusement. "Oh, it was quite the lark at first. Toby came home one day, full of excitement about this bet he'd made with Harry, a friend of his. I thought he was pulling my leg, truth be told. A fortune-teller? My Toby?" She paused, taking a sip of her tea. "But then I saw him at work during those first fairs. It was like watching a master craftsman. He had this gift, you see. He could put people at ease, and make them feel heard and understood. Before long, word spread, and more customers turned up."

Watson nodded encouragingly. "And that's when he decided to leave the theatre?"

"Yes," Mrs Knight replied. "It wasn't an easy decision. We'd both worked there for years. But the opportunity was too good to pass up. I was happy to leave my position as well, though I do miss my friends there sometimes."

Holmes' attention never left the woman's face. Even though he already knew the answer, he asked, "And what is your role in this new venture, Mrs Knight?"

Mrs Knight straightened in her chair, a hint of pride in her voice. "I manage the front of house, as it were. I greet the clients, show them to the waiting area, and offer them refreshments. And I handle the money, of course. Toby's never had a head for figures."

"I see," Holmes said. "And tell me, do you find that your husband's clientele tends to be predominantly female?"

The change in the woman's demeanour was subtle but unmistakable. Her smile tightened ever so slightly, and a flicker of something - annoyance? concern? - passed across her eyes.

"Yes," she said, her voice noticeably cooler. "We do see more women than men. Some of them have become quite devoted to Toby's services."

Watson repeated, "Devoted?"

Mrs Knight said, "Perhaps overly so. There are a few who turn up far too regularly for my liking. They seem to have trouble distinguishing between Toby's professional persona and his real self." She glowered at the window as though expecting to see those particular women walking past.

Holmes asked Mrs Knight to elaborate on the women, and how they act in front of her husband.

Mrs Knight replied, "Well, I can't give you names, of course. But one comes to mind immediately. A widow who has taken to visiting Toby at least twice a week. Always dressed to the nines, she is, with her fancy hats and silk gloves. She hangs on his every word, laughing at the slightest thing he says. And the way she looks at him! Her eyes full of adoration! I think she's in love with him."

Holmes' eyebrow arched. "And how does she treat you, Mrs Knight?"

"Like I'm nothing more than a maid. 'Fetch me a glass of water, girl,' she'll say.' As if I'm not even worthy of a proper name."

"I see," Holmes said. "Are there others?"

Mrs Knight nodded vigorously. "A young woman who has only recently turned twenty. When she arrives, she acts as if she owns the place. As soon as she's had one reading with Toby, she immediately orders me to book another with him. Says she needs Toby's 'special insight' into her future."

Watson frowned. "And does your husband oblige her?"

"He tries not to," Mrs Knight said, her voice tight. "But she's persistent. Just last week, I caught her heading towards Toby's coat which was hung up. She had a note in her hand and was trying to slip it into Toby's coat pocket when she thought I wasn't looking."

"By Jove!" Watson declared. "That is completely unacceptable. How did you handle that situation?"

Mrs Knight's eyes flashed. "I snatched it away before she could leave it, of course. Told her that if she had any messages for my husband, she could give them to me directly."

"A reasonable response," Holmes nodded. "Are there any other clients who stand out in your mind?"

"There is one more. One of Toby's wealthier clients. She's taken to bringing Toby gifts. Expensive ones, too. Silk ties, gold cufflinks, even a pocket watch once. Toby tries to refuse them, but the woman is insistent. Says they're just tokens of her appreciation for his 'invaluable guidance'."

Holmes asked, "And how does this woman treat you, Mrs Knight?"

"Like I'm not even there. She'll sweep in, all perfume and furs, and it's 'Toby, darling' this and 'my dear Mr Knight' that. She barely spares me a glance, and when she does, it's with this look of pity, I suppose. As if she can't fathom why Toby would be married to someone like me."

Watson's expression softened. "That must be very difficult for you, Mrs Knight."

She nodded, blinking rapidly. "It is. I know Toby doesn't encourage it, but well, it's hard not to feel a bit invisible sometimes." She sighed, her gaze drifting to the window again. "Sometimes I find myself missing those early days at the theatre. Life was simpler then. Just the two of us, working behind the scenes, no one paying us much mind."

Holmes and Watson exchanged a glance, both noting the wistful tone in the woman's voice.

Holmes glanced around the room and said, "Mrs Knight, your home is quite charming. You've created a most inviting atmosphere here."

Mrs Knight's face lit up with pride, her earlier distress momentarily forgotten. "Oh, thank you. We're so pleased with it. It's a far cry from our previous lodgings, I can tell you that."

Holmes said, "I'd be most interested to hear more about your former residence, if you don't mind sharing."

Mrs Knight answered, "Well, it was nothing like this, I can assure you. We were in a rather shabby part of town, you see. The landlord, Mr Ellis, was rather a rough sort. He's a dreadful man. Greedy to the core. He charged us far too much for those poorly maintained lodgings. Always promising to make repairs, but never following through. He wasn't pleased when Toby started his new business, and said it would bring the wrong sort of people around. But then he changed his tune when he realised how much money Toby would be making. He demanded a cut of Toby's earnings. He said it was only fair since Toby was running a business out of his property. We paid him, of course. We didn't want any trouble. But it never seemed to be enough for him. He kept asking for more."

Watson said, "He sounds like a most disagreeable man. How did Mr Ellis react when you gave your notice to leave?"

Mrs Knight paled. "He wasn't pleased. Not at all. He made some threats to me, actually. I never told Toby about that. I didn't want to worry him, you see."

Holmes asked, "Threats, what sort of threats?"

"He said we shouldn't get too pleased about our rise to fame. That things could change for the worse at any moment. The way he said it, oh, it chilled me to the bone."

Holmes said, "Would you be willing to provide us with the address of your former lodgings? It may prove useful in our investigation."

Mrs Knight nodded eagerly and gave them the address of a house off Whitechapel Road.

Holmes stood and said, "Thank you for your time, Mrs Knight. And the tea. We will proceed with our investigation."

Mrs Knight rose and led them out of the room. Before she closed the door on them, she gave Holmes a small smile and said, "Mr Holmes, are you sure my husband is okay?"

Holmes answered, "He is. With Dr Watson's help, I intend to solve his problem very soon. Good day to you." With a smile, he tipped his hat in farewell and walked away.

Watson added his reassuring smile to the woman and followed Holmes along the street.

Chapter 5

Holmes and Watson caught a cab to the former home of Mr and Mrs Knight with the intention of seeking out their ex-landlord, or a neighbour who would be willing to give them information about Mr Ellis and his possible whereabouts.

They arrived at a row of dilapidated tenements that lined a narrow street. After exiting the cab, they approached the house where Mr Knight and his wife had lived. It was in a sorry state of disrepair. Paint peeled from the door in great strips, exposing weathered wood beneath. Several windows were cracked or boarded up entirely, and the front steps sagged ominously.

Holmes took in every detail of the rundown structure. "Well, Watson, it appears Mrs Knight was not exaggerating about the state of their former lodgings."

Before Watson could respond, a portly man with a ruddy complexion and a threadbare coat hurried towards them, a wide smile plastered across his face.

"Good afternoon! Might you be interested in some lodgings? I'm Mr Ellis, the landlord here."

Holmes said, "Good afternoon, Mr Ellis. We were just admiring your property."

Ellis beamed, gesturing expansively towards the building. "Ah, you have got a discerning eye, sir! It's a fine establishment, if I do say so myself. Why, I've got a vacancy right now that would suit you gentlemen perfectly. You could move in straight away!"

"How very convenient," Holmes said. "And what would be the monthly rate for such accommodation?"

Ellis' eyes narrowed slightly as he looked them up and down, taking in their well-tailored suits and polished shoes. After a moment's calculation, he named a sum that made Watson's eyes widen in disbelief.

Holmes, however, merely smiled. "I see. Most interesting. However, Mr Ellis, I'm afraid we're not here about lodgings. We're actually here on a matter concerning a former tenant of yours – a Mr Knight."

The change in Ellis' demeanour was instantaneous and dramatic. His jovial smile vanished, replaced by a scowl of pure venom. "Knight?" he spat. "That ungrateful wretch? What's he been saying about me, then?"

Holmes held up a placating hand. "We're simply making inquiries. Perhaps you could tell us about your experiences with Mr Knight as a tenant?"

Ellis' face flushed an even deeper shade of red. "Experiences? I'll tell you about my experiences! That man betrayed me, plain and simple. After everything I did for him!"

Watson interjected, "Everything you did for him?"

"Aye!" Ellis nodded vigorously. "I went out of my way to accommodate his business. Turning a blind eye to all sorts coming and going at all hours. And how does he repay my kindness? By running off to greener pastures the moment he starts making a bit of money."

Holmes nodded thoughtfully. "I see. And this business of Mr Knight's, did it cause trouble with the other tenants?"

Ellis waved a dismissive hand. "Not that I know of. I run a respectable establishment here, I do. But for Knight, I made allowances and let him use his lodgings for business. More fool me." An undeniable smirk appeared on his face. "Knight will get his comeuppance, mark my words. No one makes a fool of Jeremiah Ellis and gets away with it."

Watson asked, "What do you mean by that, Mr Ellis?"

Ellis shook his head. "Never you mind about that. What's done is done, and what's to come... well, that's between me and Mr Knight, isn't it?"

Holmes studied the man intently. "Mr Ellis, if you have any information about potential harm coming to Mr Knight or his business, I strongly advise you to share it with us now."

Ellis' face darkened. "I've nothing more to say on the matter. Now, if you gentlemen aren't interested in lodgings, I'll bid you good day." With that, he turned on his heel and strode away, leaving Holmes and Watson standing on the pavement.

Chapter 6

The gas lamps flickered to life as Holmes and Watson made their way back to Baker Street, the evening shadows lengthening around them. The bustling streets of London gradually quietened as they walked, the day's business giving way to the hush of nightfall.

"Well, Watson," Holmes said as they turned onto Baker Street, "what do you make of our day's investigations?"

Watson considered the question. "I'm not sure what to make of it yet. We've certainly got some suspects."

They arrived at 221B and went inside. They climbed the steps to their rooms, where Mrs Hudson had left a tray of sandwiches and a pot of tea. Holmes poured them each a cup and they settled into their armchairs before the fire.

Holmes took a sip of his tea and then said, "Let us review what we know. We have Mr Ellis, the former landlord, who seems to harbour a great deal of resentment towards our client."

"He certainly didn't mince his words," Watson said. "That business about Knight getting his 'comeuppance' was rather ominous."

Holmes nodded. "Quite so. Ellis is certainly holding a grudge, and he strikes me as a man who might resort to underhanded tactics if he felt wronged."

"But how would he manage to interfere with Knight's predictions?" Watson asked. "He doesn't seem the type to have inside knowledge of Knight's clients or their affairs."

"A valid point," Holmes conceded. "Which brings us to our next suspect: Mrs Knight herself."

Watson said, "But she seemed so supportive of her husband's endeavours."

"On the surface, perhaps," Holmes said. "But remember what Mr Matthews told us about her jealous streak. And did you notice how her expression hardened when we asked about Mr Knight's female clients?"

Watson nodded slowly. "Yes, I did observe that. But surely she wouldn't sabotage her husband's business?"

"Jealousy can drive people to extreme actions, my dear Watson," Holmes said. "If she felt threatened by these women, which it seems she did, she might see it as a way to protect her marriage."

They fell silent for a moment, each lost in thought.

Watson broke the silence. "What about any rivals? Could another fortune-teller be behind this, trying to discredit Knight?"

"It's possible. Knight's success might well have drawn clients away from other practitioners in the area. To find evidence of that, a visit to other fortune-tellers would be needed. Something which I am not prepared to do at this point."

"Oh, I don't know. A visit to at least a couple of them could be informative," Watson said, a hint of amusement in his voice. "Perhaps we could have our own fortunes told while we're at it."

Holmes shot him a withering look. "I think not, Watson. Dealing with one fortune-teller is quite enough for me, thank you. I have no desire to subject myself to more of that nonsense."

Watson chuckled. "Fair enough. What do you suggest, then?"

"I believe our best course of action is to speak with Knight's clients next. Those who received premonitions that came true in an unfortunate manner. If we can understand exactly how those predictions manifested, we might uncover some clue as to how they were manipulated –

if indeed they were. I'm not entirely convinced on that matter yet."

"That seems a sensible approach," Watson agreed. "Shall we set out first thing in the morning?"

Holmes said, "Yes. As we only have their business addresses, we'll set out as soon as those workplaces open for the day."

Watson smiled, a mischievous glint in his eye. "You know, Holmes, in some ways, your profession isn't all that different from fortune-telling."

Holmes lowered his teacup. "I beg your pardon?"

"Well, think about it," Watson said, warming to his theme. "You read a great deal about a person as soon as you see them – their appearance, their attire, their manner of speech. You deduce their past and present circumstances from your observations."

"That is simple logic and deduction," Holmes protested. "Not mystical nonsense."

"Of course," Watson said, his smile widening. "But then you tell the client that you will solve their problem. Isn't that a kind of premonition?"

Holmes stared at his friend for a moment, then burst into laughter. "I suppose you have me there. Perhaps there are some superficial similarities. But I assure you, I have no intention of setting up shop as a fortune-teller."

"More's the pity," Watson said. "I dare say you'd make a fortune."

"I'll stick to detective work, thank you very much," Holmes said, still smiling. "Now, we should get some rest. Tomorrow promises to be an interesting day."

Chapter 7

The following morning, Holmes and Watson made their way to the textile factory where the first of Knight's clients, Miss Gwendolyn Fairchild, worked.

Upon arrival, they were greeted by the factory manager, a friendly gentleman named Mr Wilkins. He led them through a cacophonous workroom, where rows of women hunched over clattering looms.

As they walked along, the manager asked Holmes if Miss Fairchild was in some sort of bother. He pointed out she had been at the factory for over five years and was one of his most diligent workers.

Holmes assured him Miss Fairchild wasn't in any bother at all, and they merely wished to talk to her about a private matter concerning one of their clients.

"Miss Fairchild! A word, if you please," Mr Wilkins called over the din.

A young woman with tired eyes and calloused hands approached, wiping her brow with a threadbare handkerchief.

"These gentlemen would like a word. Take your break now. You can use my office."

Miss Fairchild gave Holmes and Watson a curious look and led them into a small, stuffy office. She perched nervously on a wooden chair. Holmes and Watson took seats opposite her.

After introducing himself and Watson, Holmes said, "We understand you had a reading with Mr Toby Knight. Could you tell us about it, please?"

Miss Fairchild answered, "Of course. I'd saved up for months to see him. Some of the other women who work here had been to see him and said he was accurate. I wanted to know about my future, if things would ever get better." Spots of colour appeared on her cheeks. "Well, what I really wanted to know was if I would meet the man I'm going to fall in love with and marry soon."

"And what did he tell you?" Holmes asked.

"He listened, really listened. He made me feel like I mattered. He said I should stay positive, that romance was on the horizon. Then he told me to be open to all sorts of suitors, even those I mightn't normally consider."

Watson nodded encouragingly. "And did you follow his advice?"

A shadow crossed Miss Fairchild's face. "I did. That's when the trouble started."

She went on to explain how, emboldened by Knight's words, she'd accepted an invitation from a charming man named Edward Baxenden who approached her in a cafe one day. "He wasn't my usual sort, but then I remembered what Mr Knight said."

"How did things progress with Mr Baxenden?" Holmes asked.

"Oh, it was like a dream at first. He'd turn up for our dates in the finest clothes, and always had money for dinners and shows. Edward said he was in shipping and was very successful. After a few weeks, he told me he loved me and had done since the moment he first saw me. I was over the moon. I thought all my dreams were coming true." She stopped talking and looked down at her dress.

"But something changed?" Watson prompted gently.

She nodded and looked back up. "I took Edward home to meet my mother. It was his idea and he said he wanted to speak to her about a personal matter. I thought that meant he was going to propose soon, so I agreed.

"Well, Edward charmed my mother, just as he had charmed me. We left him in the living room for a few minutes while we went into the kitchen to prepare food and drink. When we came back, he was gone. And so were our savings. We kept them in an old tin on a shelf behind some ornaments. He took everything. All the money Mother and I had worked years to save. I know we should have put the money in the bank, but Mother doesn't trust them. She said our home was safer."

Watson's face creased with sympathy. "I'm so sorry that happened to you. Did you try to find him?"

Miss Fairchild laughed bitterly. "Of course. But everything he'd told me was a lie. The address he'd given me didn't exist. I asked around and no one in the shipping business had ever heard of him. It was all a sham."

"And you believe Mr Knight is responsible for this?" Holmes asked, his tone carefully neutral.

"Who else?" Miss Fairchild's voice rose with anger. "He's the one who told me to be open to different types of men. If it weren't for him, I'd never have given Edward a second glance. And now look where I am. Worse off than before, with all our savings gone." She paused, her eyes narrowing. "Sometimes I wonder if Mr Knight hired that man himself. To steal from me. I foolishly told Mr Knight about how I'd taken money from my savings to pay for a reading for him, and somehow, he managed to get me to admit where my savings were kept."

"Do you have any evidence to support your claim that Mr Knight is behind this deception?" Holmes asked.

She shook her head. "No, I don't. It's just a feeling. But who else is to blame? He filled my head with false hope and made me ignore my own good sense. I went back to his house after the money had been stolen, and I told Mr Knight it was all his fault. He was upset, or so he said, but he wouldn't accept responsibility. He said I should tell the police. Which I did. But they didn't seem very interested."

Holmes said, "Miss Fairchild, could you describe Mr Baxenden for us?"

Miss Fairchild replied, "Well, he was handsome. Tall, I'd say about six feet. He had dark hair, thick and wavy."

"And his face?" Holmes asked.

"He had a full beard and moustache," she replied, her hands unconsciously gesturing around her own face. "It was neatly trimmed, dark like his hair. Made him look distinguished, you know?"

Watson nodded encouragingly, making notes of her description.

"His eyes were blue," Miss Fairchild continued, her gaze distant as she recalled the man who had deceived her. "They could be very warm when he smiled, but thinking back now, there was something cold about them too."

"What of his build?" Holmes asked. "Was he stout, thin?"

"Of medium build," Miss Fairchild said. "Not overly muscular, mind you, but he looked strong. He carried himself with confidence, always stood up straight."

"And his manner of dress?" Holmes inquired.

"Always impeccable. Fine suits, polished shoes. He wore a gold pocket watch on a chain. He said it was a family heirloom."

Holmes asked for more information about the mystery man, and once Miss Fairchild had done her best to answer, he thanked her for her time.

He rose from his chair, Watson following suit.

The young woman looked up at them, a glimmer of hope in her tired eyes. "Do you think you'll be able to find Edward? To get our money back?"

Holmes' expression softened slightly. "We shall certainly do our utmost, Miss Fairchild. While I cannot promise success, I assure you we will investigate this matter thoroughly."

Watson added, "If you should remember anything else, please don't hesitate to contact us."

Miss Fairchild nodded.

With that, Holmes and Watson took their leave, stepping back into the clamour of the factory floor. They swiftly made their way through the factory and back onto the busy street, which seemed like a haven of tranquillity in comparison.

Watson turned to Holmes. "As sorry as I am to hear about Miss Fairchild's bad luck with Mr Baxenden, I'm not sure Mr Knight's prediction is to blame. What do you think, Holmes?"

Holmes answered, "I'm not certain either, my dear Watson. Let us see what those other two clients have to say. If a pattern emerges, then we'll know something is amiss. Let's track down the disgraced journalist, Cyril Thorne, and hear his story."

Chapter 8

A while later, Holmes and Watson arrived at the newspaper offices where Cyril Thorne had worked. Once inside, they explained to the receptionist that they would like to speak to Mr Thorne on a matter of some importance, and would like to know where to find him, if that was possible.

The obliging receptionist took them to a cramped office where a middle-aged man with ink-stained fingers sat behind a desk piled high with papers. She introduced them to him and gave the reason for their visit. She smiled at Holmes and Watson before walking away.

The man said, "A pleasure to meet you both. I'm Thaddeus Gifford. Take a seat and tell me more about your request."

Holmes sat down and got straight to the point. "We're investigating a matter concerning Cyril Thorne and need to speak to him. We understand he used to work here."

Gifford said, "Ah, poor Cyril. Terrible business, that."

"Could you tell us more about him? His work ethics, perhaps?" Holmes asked.

Gifford leaned back in his chair, which creaked under his weight. "Cyril was one of our best. Meticulous, he was. He always triple-checked his sources. That's why it was such a shock when that article of his turned out to be complete rubbish. It wasn't like Cyril at all to publish something like that. He had built up such a reputation for reliability. I still don't understand why he did it, I really don't.

"When the article came out, we were visited by the politician in question and told in no uncertain terms that we had to fire Cyril. Not only that, we had to print an apology and pay the man compensation. We had no choice but to let Cyril go. We're still trying to recover from the damage to our reputation. Cyril was heartbroken, and apologised profusely, but what could we do? We couldn't let him stay. Not after what he'd done."

Holmes asked, "Do you know where we might find Mr Thorne now?"

Gifford nodded towards the window. "If he's not at home, you'll likely find him at The Broken Quill. It's a pub just down the street. He's been drowning his sorrows there most days since he was let go."

After getting Thorne's home address in case they needed it, Holmes and Watson thanked Gifford for his time and made their way out of the office.

As they stepped onto the street, Holmes said, "This is a curious one, Watson. A man known for his thoroughness suddenly publishes an article without proper verification. It doesn't add up. Something doesn't feel right. Let's see if Mr Thorne is drowning his sorrows, as Mr Gifford stated."

They walked briskly down the street and soon located The Broken Quill. The pub was a squat, weathered building with a faded sign swinging in the breeze.

Inside, the air was thick with tobacco smoke and the low murmur of conversation. Holmes scanned the room, quickly spotting a dejected figure hunched over a table in the corner. He was the only person sitting alone.

They approached the man, who looked up at them with bloodshot eyes. His clothes were rumpled, and a day's growth of stubble shadowed his chin.

"Mr Thorne?" Holmes inquired gently.

The man nodded, gesturing vaguely at the empty chairs. "Take a seat, gents. Might as well join me in my misery."

As they sat, Watson noticed the array of empty glasses on the table. Thorne caught his glance and chuckled mirthlessly.

"Don't worry. I'm not so far gone that I can't string a sentence together. What can I do for you?"

Holmes introduced himself and Watson, and then said, "We're investigating a matter concerning Mr Toby Knight. We understand you had a reading with him."

Thorne's face darkened. "That charlatan. I should've known better than to listen to him. I should never have gone to him in the first place."

"Could you tell us about your experience?" Watson asked.

Thorne took a long swig from his glass before replying. "I've never been to a fortune-teller before. I thought it was all nonsense. But my career was in a rut and I needed something to shake things up."

Holmes asked, "And what did Mr Knight tell you?"

"He told me to widen my circles. To visit places where I hadn't been before. Talk to people I normally wouldn't meet. And then, I'd have more chance of finding a big story." Thorne laughed bitterly. "Well, I certainly did that. I started venturing into parts of London I'd never bothered with before. Seedier areas. And that's where I met that informer who gave me the story. Or rather, he met me. He approached me out of the shadows, almost as if he was waiting for me."

Holmes said, "Who was this man?"

"I never got his name. He said he worked for an MP and claimed the man was corrupt. He said he'd recognised me from being in this pub with my colleagues and heard my name being mentioned. He'd read some of my articles in the newspaper and said I was the right journalist for his story. The man offered me documents; all evidence of so-called illegal activities." Thorne gave them a small smile. "It sounded like the story of a lifetime. I remember thinking that Toby Knight had given me the right advice after all, and was glad I had gone to see him."

Watson said, "Can you describe this man?"

Thorne nodded, his brow furrowed in concentration. "He was about six feet tall, I'd say. Light brown hair, no beard. Well dressed. Spoke like a gent, if you know what I mean. He wore thick glasses, so I couldn't see what colour his eyes were, but I don't think they were dark. He seemed respectable and trustworthy."

"And the documents?" Holmes said. "What did they look like?"

Thorne answered, "They looked genuine. I normally check my sources thoroughly, but the man said it was imperative that I publish the article soon because the MP in question was about to leave the country with his ill-gotten gains. But, as you probably know by now, the documents turned out to be forgeries. Clever ones, but forgeries nonetheless. By the time I realised, it was too late. The damage was done."

Watson said, "Did you blame Mr Knight for your misfortunes?"

"I certainly did!" Thorne exclaimed. "If he hadn't told me to widen my circles, I never would have gone to the seedier parts of London. It was all his fault, and I told him so. He said he was sorry about what had happened to me, but there was nothing he could do. He refunded the money I'd paid for my reading, but that won't pay my rent, will it? My reputation is ruined, and it's all because of Toby Knight."

Holmes said, "Mr Thorne, I believe you may have been the victim of an elaborate scheme. We're investigating a similar incident, and your story fits a pattern we're seeing. I know that can't be much comfort to you at this stage, and I am truly sorry for your misfortunes."

A glimmer of hope appeared in Thorne's bloodshot eyes. "Mr Holmes, if you manage to find whoever is behind this scheme and get justice, then I'll be happy with that. It won't get my job back, or restore my reputation, but I'd like to see whoever tricked me brought to justice. Will you let me know how you get on?"

"Of course," Holmes said. He rose from his chair and thanked Thorne for his help.

Thorne raised his glass and wished them luck.

Holmes and Watson left the pub.

Watson said, "So, there is a pattern forming here. A mysterious man who is targeting those who've had readings with Mr Knight. And he's ensuring that their predictions are taking a turn for the worse. What are your thoughts on this, Holmes?"

"You are right about a pattern emerging. Our investigation is not yet complete, though. Let's speak to the final client of Mr Knight's. The investment banker. Mr Endicott, wasn't it?"

Watson quickly consulted his notes. "That's right. He works at Roseberry Investment Bank on Threadneedle Street. Shall we walk or hail a cab?"

"I'd prefer to walk," Holmes replied. "Walking always helps me to think."

"Rightio," Watson said, and the two of them strode along the street, Holmes silent as they walked.

Chapter 9

Holmes and Watson stood before the imposing façade of Roseberry Investment Bank on Threadneedle Street. The building's stone exterior exuded an air of wealth and respectability, its large windows reflecting the bustling street below.

As they entered the marble-floored lobby, the din of the London streets faded away, replaced by the hushed tones of people discussing financial matters. A smartly dressed clerk approached them, his polished shoes clicking on the marble floor.

"May I help you?"

Holmes removed his hat. "We're here to see Mr Leonard Endicott. The name is Sherlock Holmes, and this is my colleague, Dr Watson."

The clerk's eyebrows rose slightly at the mention of Holmes' name. "One moment, please."

He disappeared down a corridor, returning moments later with a nod. "Mr Endicott will see you now. Please follow me."

They were led through a maze of corridors, past offices where men in expensive suits pored over ledgers and conversed with clients. Finally, they arrived at a heavy oak door with a brass nameplate: 'Leonard Endicott'.

The clerk knocked and ushered them in. Mr Endicott rose from behind a massive mahogany desk, his tailored suit speaking of wealth and success. He was a man in his fifties, with greying hair at his temples. There was a weariness about him as though he hadn't slept well for many nights.

"Mr Holmes, Dr Watson, please, have a seat. What can I do for you?"

As they settled into the plush leather chairs, Holmes said, "Mr Endicott, we're investigating a matter concerning Toby Knight. We understand you had a reading with him."

Endicott sighed. "Ah, yes. That fortune-teller. I suppose I have only myself to blame for listening to such nonsense."

"Could you tell us about your experience?"

Endicott began, "It all started at Wilton's Café. I was there one afternoon, enjoying my usual cup of Earl Grey, when I overheard the most peculiar conversation."

He went on to describe how a man and woman at the next table were singing the praises of a new fortune-teller called Toby Knight who was becoming extremely successful. The couple spoke with such conviction about Knight's abilities that Endicott found himself leaning closer to catch every word. Despite his usual scepticism towards such matters, he felt a spark of intrigue ignite within him. The way they described Night's uncanny insights and spot-on predictions made Endicott wonder if there might be something to this fortune-telling business after all. He struck up a conversation with them and asked where they could find Knight.

"I've never put much stock in fortune-tellers, you understand. In my line of work, we deal with facts and figures, not crystal balls and tarot cards. But something about their conviction intrigued me. And, I don't mind admitting, my business dealings had been lacklustre. It's been a while since I brought in any new clients, and my colleagues were starting to notice. I knew I had to do something to change that."

"So you decided to visit Mr Knight?" Watson asked.

Endicott nodded. "I made an appointment and went to see him. The whole experience was unsettling. He seemed to know things about me, about my work, just by looking at me and asking a couple of questions. When I mentioned my business dealings and asked if I should take more risks, he advised caution and said I should trust my instincts. He told me to be wary of any unnecessary risks."

Holmes asked, "And what happened after your reading?"

"I returned to Wilton Café a few weeks after that reading. There was a new investment opportunity I'd been considering and I needed time to think about it. But Knight's words echoed in my mind and I wasn't sure what to do about the matter. As I sat there, wrestling with my decision, who should I spot but the gentleman from the couple I'd overheard before.

"He asked if I'd been to see Knight, and I said I had. I didn't tell him what Knight had told me, but he was happy to tell me the reading he'd had with Knight. The strange thing was, this man was in the investment business too, and Knight had also told him to be wary of taking risks. The man heeded his advice and refused to take part in a new investment that had arisen at his place of work. Which proved fortunate, because his colleagues went ahead, and days later they suffered tremendous losses because of it.

"It was all too much of a coincidence. I decided to err on the side of caution and I passed on the investment."

"A decision you came to regret, I take it?" Holmes said.

Endicott's fist clenched on the desk. "Regret doesn't begin to cover it, Mr Holmes. That investment turned out to be one of the most lucrative opportunities of the decade. My colleagues who invested, well, let's just say they're now in a position to buy out my share of the firm if they wished. So far, they have taken pity on me and haven't gone ahead with that course of action. But I'm not in the habit of receiving pity. It doesn't sit well with me. This whole situation has arisen because of Knight's words. But perhaps I am to blame, too, for believing him."

Watson asked, "Mr Endicott, this man you encountered at the café, can you describe him?"

Endicott replied, "Tall chap, about six feet. Light brown hair, clean-shaven. Respectable sort. Well dressed."

"And what about his eye colour?" Watson asked.

Endicott said, "I've no idea. I remember he was wearing spectacles, though."

"Mr Endicott," Holmes said, "I believe you may have been the victim of an elaborate scheme."

Endicott's eyes widened. "You mean, this wasn't just bad luck?"

"That remains to be seen," Holmes replied. "But I assure you, we will get to the bottom of this matter."

Mr Endicott asked if they would let him know how their investigation went. Holmes assured him they would.

As they left the bank, Watson said, "The similarities in these cases are undeniable."

Holmes gave Watson a direct look and said, "How tall do you think Mr Knight is?"

Watson considered the matter. "I'd say at least six foot, maybe a bit more." As he said the words, his face lit up in understanding. "You don't think Knight is behind all this, do you, Holmes?"

"I told you from the beginning, my dear Watson, that I didn't trust him. And from what Mr Endicott has told us about his visits to that café, this unnamed man may be working with a woman, which only means one thing."

"That Mrs Knight is in on this scheme too." Watson shook his head. "But why would they do this? How does it benefit them? And why get us involved?"

"All good questions, my dear friend," Holmes said. "Let's pay a visit to Mr Knight and see what he has to say."

Chapter 10

Not long later, Holmes and Watson approached the house of Mr Knight. A small queue of people, mostly women, stood outside the door, shifting impatiently from foot to foot.

"Good heavens," Holmes muttered, his voice tinged with exasperation. "It seems Mr Knight is presently open for business. And despite what he told us, his business appears to be thriving."

Watson nodded, observing the varied expressions on the waiting faces. "Perhaps we should have made an appointment."

Holmes grunted in reply and reluctantly joined the queue.

Mrs Knight opened the door and ushered the waiting clients into the sitting room which had now been converted into a makeshift waiting room with rows of chairs lined up against the walls. Holmes and Watson followed the clients and found a couple of empty seats and sat down. Holmes glanced around the room, taking in the people who were awaiting a reading from Knight.

A young woman in a crisp white blouse and dark skirt sat ramrod straight, her fingers tapping a nervous rhythm on her knee. Beside her, an older gentleman with a salt-and-pepper beard stroked his chin thoughtfully, his eyes distant. In the corner, two middle-aged women whispered excitedly, their faces flushed with anticipation.

Holmes tutted to himself. He stood up and approached Mrs Knight. Keeping his voice low, he said, "Mrs Knight, I must speak with your husband immediately."

Mrs Knight replied, "I'm sorry, Mr Holmes, but these people have appointments. They've been waiting a long time for their readings."

Holmes retorted, "Then they can wait a while longer. I need to speak to your husband without any delay."

A murmur of discontent rippled through the room.

The young woman in office attire stood up, her chin jutting out defiantly. "Now see here, I've been waiting for weeks for this appointment. I need Mr Knight's advice on my career. I'm not about to let you push in front of me."

Holmes opened his mouth, clearly ready to unleash his feelings about people who visit fortune-tellers, but Watson rushed over to his side and placed a gentle hand on his friend's arm. "Perhaps we should wait our turn, Holmes," he said.

The detective's jaw clenched, but he nodded curtly. "Very well."

They returned to their seats, everyone in the room watching them.

Moments later, the whispers began.

"Isn't that Sherlock Holmes?"

"The detective? What's he doing here?"

"Maybe he needs help with a case!"

A titter of laughter rippled through the room at this last suggestion. Holmes sat rigidly, his grey eyes flashing with annoyance.

"I assure you, madam," he said icily to the woman who had spoken, "I am perfectly capable of solving my own cases without resorting to alternative methods."

Watson cleared his throat diplomatically. "We're here on official business," he explained, hoping to quell the gossip.

Mrs Knight, sensing the tension, approached Holmes and said quietly, "I'll speak to my husband as soon as he's finished with his current client. Perhaps he can see you for a few minutes before his next appointment."

Holmes nodded curtly. "Thank you, Mrs Knight. That would be most appreciated." He ignored the waves of hostility that came his way.

Minutes later, the sound of a distant door opening could be heard, and a middle-aged woman entered the waiting room, her eyes shining with unshed tears.

"It was wonderful," she said to no one in particular. "He knew things... things no one could possibly know. He's truly gifted." Smiling, she left the room with whatever wonderful information Mr Knight had given her.

The next client stood, ready for her reading. Mrs Knight intercepted her and said, "I'm terribly sorry, but there is a matter that needs my husband's attention. It won't take long, I promise."

Ignoring the grumbles of protest, Mrs Knight beckoned to Holmes and Watson. "Gentlemen, if you'll follow me."

As Holmes and Watson rose from their seats, the young woman in office attire called out, "I hope Mr Knight can help you with your case, Mr Holmes!"

Holmes paused. For a moment, it seemed he might retort, but instead, he simply nodded and walked out of the room, Watson close behind.

Mrs Knight led them down the hallway and into a side room. She opened the door and told her husband that Mr

Holmes and Dr Watson wished to talk to him. She stepped to one side, allowing Holmes and Watson to enter. Mrs Knight gave them a nod and walked away, closing the door behind her.

Holmes and Watson were immediately enveloped by an atmosphere thick with mystery and intrigue. The room was a masterpiece of theatrical design, carefully crafted to evoke a sense of the otherworldly.

Heavy velvet drapes in deep burgundy hung from ceiling to floor, obscuring any natural light. The air was heavy with the scent of exotic incense, wisps of smoke curling lazily through the dim room. Ornate brass lamps cast a warm, flickering glow, creating dancing shadows in the corners.

In the centre of the room stood a massive oak table, its surface covered with a midnight blue cloth embroidered with golden stars and mystical symbols. A crystal ball was artfully arranged alongside tarot cards and rune stones.

Seated behind this impressive display was Mr Knight, almost unrecognisable from the unassuming man they had met previously. He was resplendent in a flowing robe of midnight blue, adorned with silver moons and stars that seemed to shimmer in the lamplight. A matching turban, complete with a large, glittering costume jewel, sat atop his head. His fingers, adorned with numerous rings, rested lightly on the table.

"Good grief," Watson muttered under his breath.

Holmes said to the fortune-teller, "I see Mrs Knight's skills as a seamstress have been put to good use, Mr Knight. Your costume is quite elaborate."

Knight shifted uncomfortably. "Yes, well, it's what the clients expect."

"Indeed." Holmes's tone was dry. "Shall we discuss the matter at hand?"

Knight nodded, gesturing to two ornate chairs opposite him. "Please, sit."

As they settled into the chairs, which were far less comfortable than they appeared, Holmes said, "Mr Knight, we've made some disturbing discoveries in our investigation."

"What sort of discoveries?"

"It seems there's a connection between your clients who experienced those unfortunate predictions. A man has been approaching them, feeding them information that aligns with your readings."

Knight's eyes widened. "Good Lord. Are you certain?"

Holmes replied, "Quite certain. We have descriptions from three separate incidents. There are undeniable similarities."

"Can you tell me what those are?"

Holmes nodded. "He's described as being tall, around six feet. However, his appearance seems to change slightly with each encounter. In two instances, we have been assured that his eyes were blue." He fell silent, letting his words sink in.

Knight paled visibly. "You must suspect me, then. That I'm this mystery man."

"The thought had occurred to us," Holmes admitted. "You certainly have the theatrical background to pull off such disguises. And you would have intimate knowledge of your clients' readings."

"But why would I do that?"

Holmes said, "You would benefit greatly from these predictions coming true. It would cement your reputation as a genuine fortune teller."

Knight nodded slowly. "Yes, I can see why you'd think that. And I admit, it does sound plausible when you lay it out like that."

"But you deny it?" Holmes asked, his eyes narrowing.

"Absolutely," Knight said firmly. "I may be a charlatan in your eyes, Mr Holmes, but I'm not a criminal. I've never approached any of my clients outside of these rooms, nor have I enlisted anyone else to do so."

"Nonetheless, Mr Knight, it appears someone is approaching your clients, or rather, they are targeting them based on the readings you've given."

Knight's brow furrowed. "But how? My readings are private, confidential."

"Who would know about these readings?" Holmes asked.

Knight shook his head, bewildered. "No one. Unless the clients themselves share the information with friends or family."

A sudden movement from beyond the door caught Holmes' attention. Mrs Knight's voice drifted through, clear and melodious, as she spoke to someone.

Holmes said, "It appears that this door allows sounds to pass through easily. Anyone standing outside that door could overhear your consultations. Does your wife often pass by this door?"

Knight exclaimed, "Surely you don't think Ava is involved in this!"

"One of your clients mentioned seeing the mystery man with a woman at a café meeting," Holmes said quietly.

Knight's face flushed with indignation. "That's preposterous! Why on earth would Ava do such a thing?"

"Perhaps you could tell us," Watson interjected gently.

Knight shook his head vehemently. "No, absolutely not. Ava has been nothing but supportive of my work. She'd never do anything to jeopardise it."

Holmes leaned back in his chair, his eyes never leaving Knight's face. "Someone has become privy to these private readings, Mr Knight. Or certainly, the readings that you gave to those three clients of yours. When exactly did those take place?"

Knight replied, "They were all on the same day, actually. A Friday. It was about a month ago. I remember it because I was ending my workday early. I had somewhere to be." He stopped speaking and the colour drained from his face.

Holmes said, "Mr Knight, what have you remembered? You must tell us."

Knight swallowed hard, his voice trembling slightly as he shared his new information. As he spoke, Holmes' expression changed from interest to urgency.

"We must leave immediately," Holmes declared, rising abruptly from his chair. "Watson, come along. There's not a moment to lose."

Chapter 11

Holmes and Watson hurried through the streets of London and towards The Royal Crescent Theatre.

As they approached the theatre, they could hear the excited chatter of a crowd gathering outside. A large poster advertised the afternoon's performance, a romantic drama set in the Regency era.

They entered through the main doors, blending in with the throng of theatregoers. Holmes nudged Watson and nodded towards a door marked 'Staff Only'. Taking advantage of a moment when the usher's attention was diverted, they slipped through the door and into the backstage area.

Holmes led Watson towards a room that he'd noticed on their previous visit. It was a room where costumes were stored. The door was ajar and they heard the sound of a woman mumbling to herself.

They entered the room and were greeted by a flustered woman with greying hair pinned up in a severe bun. She was surrounded by racks of costumes and piles of fabric, her hands full of what appeared to be a half-finished cloak.

"What do you want?" she snapped, not bothering to look up from her work. "I'm busy, as you can see."

Holmes, unperturbed by her brusque manner, said smoothly, "I apologise for interrupting you, but may we ask you a few questions? It won't take long, I promise."

The woman sighed dramatically and said, "Okay, but make it quick."

After introducing himself and Watson, Holmes asked if certain items might be available in the costume department, including a gold pocket watch. She nodded and said those items were quite common. Holmes then asked if anyone could take the items freely, or if would they need her permission.

The woman raised her chin and said, "No one gets past me. I'm always here. This is my department and I don't allow anyone to come in and help themselves. Imagine the chaos if that happened! Oh no, every item that is taken out of here needs to be approved by me, I can assure you of that."

Holmes smiled, and asked if those items he'd mentioned had been taken out recently, perhaps over the last month or so.

The woman frowned. "Now that I think about it, yes, someone did ask to borrow those items. I thought it was strange considering his work, but he said he was helping one of the actors out by collecting the items for him. I had no reason to doubt him, and he always brought the items back when they were no longer needed."

"And the name of this man?" Holmes asked.

The woman gave the name.

Holmes said, "Thank you. You've been most helpful. We won't take up another precious moment of your time." He bowed his head in farewell and left the room with Watson at his side.

They made their way through the backstage corridors and soon got closer to the stage area.

"There he is," Watson said, nodding towards a figure standing near the wings.

Harry Matthews stood with his back to them, his arm wrapped around the waist of a woman in a Regency costume. She laughed at something he said. The intimacy between them was obvious, even from a distance.

As Holmes and Watson approached, the woman noticed their presence. She turned to Matthews and told him she had to go. She kissed him lightly on the cheek, and then rushed towards the stage.

Matthews' smile lingered as he watched her go, but it froze when he turned and saw Holmes and Watson walking towards him. A flicker of nervousness crossed his face, quickly masked by a welcoming grin.

"Mr Holmes, Dr Watson! What a pleasant surprise. Have you come to enjoy the show?"

Holmes shook his head. "I'm afraid not, Mr Matthews. We're here on business. Is there somewhere quiet we might talk?"

Matthews' smile faltered for a moment and Holmes saw the unease in his blue eyes. "Of course, of course. Follow me."

He led them through a maze of props and scenery, past bustling stagehands and chattering performers. Holmes took in Matthews' height and calculated him to be precisely six feet in height.

The trio came to a small room, little more than a closet, filled with paintbrushes and half-empty cans of varnish.

"It's not much," Matthews said, ushering them inside, "but it's private. Now, what can I do for you?"

Holmes said, "We've made some progress in Mr Knight's case. During our investigation, we discovered that you recently borrowed some costumes from the wardrobe department."

Matthews looked away from them. "You must be mistaken about that, Mr Holmes. Why would I want to borrow any costumes?"

Holmes continued, "We have it on good authority that you did borrow them, Mr Matthews, and you claimed you were collecting them on behalf of an actor. But I don't believe that is the case."

Matthews looked back at them. "What do you mean by that?"

Holmes explained, "We have spoken to three individuals who had readings with Mr Knight. Each of them subsequently suffered a misfortune which they attribute to Mr Knight's advice. And each of these unfortunate souls claims they were approached by a stranger who played a role in their misfortune. The descriptions of this stranger's attire match precisely with the costumes you borrowed, Mr Matthews."

Matthews shook his head. "That's just a coincidence. It must be."

"I don't believe in coincidences," Holmes said sternly. "One of the individuals we interviewed mentioned that on one occasion, the unknown man was accompanied by a woman. We couldn't help but notice you in a rather intimate conversation with a lady just moments ago. Perhaps she might be able to shed some light on those borrowed costumes?"

At the mention of the woman, Matthews' face flushed red, and his voice took on a desperate edge. "No! Leave Hetty out of this. She knows nothing about it!" She's not involved in any of this. Whatever you think I've done, Hetty is innocent."

Holmes' eyes narrowed, sensing the depth of Matthews' panic. "Your concern for Hetty is admirable, Mr Matthews. But it does make me wonder what exactly you're trying to protect her from."

The carpenter's earlier bravado had crumbled, leaving behind a man visibly wrestling with his conscience. He said, "Okay, I'll tell you everything."

Chapter 12

Harry Matthews leaned against the wall as though needing its support. He said, "I suppose you've worked it out, Mr Holmes."

Holmes nodded, his expression impassive. "I believe I have. But I'd like to hear your side of the story, if you please."

"I was happy for Toby, I really was," Matthews began. "When he first started out as a fortune-teller, I thought it was a lark. But then he got more and more successful, and I... well, I suppose I got a bit jealous. Well, more than a bit, if I'm honest.

"About a month ago, I invited Toby out for a few drinks. I thought it'd be nice to catch up with him. But as the night wore on, and we both had a few too many, Toby started bragging. At least, that's how it seemed to me at the time. He kept going on about how successful he was, how glad he was to have got away from the stage. Then he looked at me and said, 'I wouldn't like to be stuck there for life like you are, Harry. Why don't you leave? Aren't you brave enough to do that?'

"I got more and more annoyed. I kept buying Toby drinks, hoping he'd shut up, I suppose. But he just kept talking, telling me all about his clients that day, what he'd told them. And suddenly, I knew I had to take him down a peg or two. Teach him a lesson, like. It was easy, really. Toby had given me enough information about each client. All I had to do was track them down and make sure those predictions came true. But not in the way they were hoping.

"I borrowed the costumes from the wardrobe department. I got Hetty to help me with one of the charades, the one in the cafe. She thought we were just playing a harmless prank. I never told her the whole truth. She'd be so ashamed of me if she knew. But I just wanted to teach Toby a lesson. I wanted his clients to complain to him. Let him know he wasn't as amazing as he claimed. That's all."

Matthews fell silent, his confession complete. The weight of his actions seemed to press down on him, making him appear smaller in the cramped confines of the storage room.

Holmes said, "We spoke with Mr Knight before coming here. He mentioned meeting you about a month ago, though he confessed to having trouble recalling the details of that evening. It seems he imbibed more than usual, which he found rather out of character. Mr Knight vaguely remembered you purchasing all the drinks that night. More concerningly, he recalled discussing his clients from that day. This is something he assured us he never does, given the confidential nature of his work."

"I didn't force him to talk about his clients," Matthews attempted to defend himself. "He did that on his own."

"But you took advantage of that," Watson said, joining in the conversation. "Mr Knight informed us he had seen six clients that day and, to his dismay, believes he may have spoken about all of them with you."

"There were six," Matthew admitted. "I've only managed to get to three of them so far."

Watson couldn't contain his shock. "Good heavens! Have you no shame?"

Before Matthews could respond, Holmes interjected. "Mr Matthews, you must understand the gravity of your actions. You have caused a lot of hurt to innocent parties, and I'm including Mr Knight in that. There's still time to make amends for what you've done."

Matthews scowled. "And what if I deny everything? It's my word against yours."

The tense silence that followed was shattered by the sound of the door creaking open.

Hetty stepped into the cramped room, her eyes sparkling with unshed tears. "I heard everything, Harry. You can't deny what you did. It's not right. You have to confess."

Matthews turned to her. "Hetty, I can't. I'll go to prison."

She held up a hand. "I don't care about that. You have to do the right thing. I can't believe what you've done, Harry. And to think you used me as well, to trick one of those poor people. I won't stand for it. You need to tell the police everything, or we're finished."

The fight seemed to drain out of Matthews all at once. He gave Hetty a weak smile and said, "Okay. I'll do it. For you. I'll tell the police everything."

Hetty nodded, her face set in determination. She held her hand out to Matthews. "We'll go to the police station together, right now."

Holmes said to the couple, "Dr Watson and I will accompany you. I believe our testimony may prove useful in this matter."

The group left the theatre, Matthew's head low as he avoided the curious looks from the people he worked with; those people who would soon hear about the terrible things he had done.

Once Holmes and Watson had given their statements to the police, they visited each of Matthews' victims to let them know what had happened before returning back to the home of Mr and Mrs Knight.

Chapter 13

Inside 221B Baker Street a week later, Holmes reclined in his favourite armchair, his eyes closed, and Dr Watson sat at his desk, replying to some letters they'd received.

A gentle knock at the door roused them from their respective reveries.

Mrs Hudson entered. "Mr Knight to see you," she announced, ushering in the visitor before swiftly retreating.

Holmes straightened in his chair. "Mr Knight, please, take a seat," he said, gesturing to the chair opposite him. "What brings you here today?"

Knight settled into the offered seat. "Mr Holmes, Dr Watson, I wanted to express my deepest gratitude for your help in this matter. I'm well aware of your reservations about my profession, Mr Holmes, which makes your assistance all the more appreciated."

Holmes waved a dismissive hand. "The safety of the public was at stake. Personal opinions must be set aside in such circumstances. I'm just glad we solved your case."

Knight said, "I'm still in shock over what Harry did. But I can't help but feel somewhat responsible for what transpired. When I think back to that evening with Harry, I fear I may have been overzealous in my boasting. Perhaps if I'd been more modest, none of this would have happened."

"True friends rejoice in one another's successes, Mr Knight," Holmes declared. "They do not allow jealousy to corrupt their affections or drive them to harmful actions. Take my good friend, Dr Watson. I am constantly impressed by his accounts of our adventures in the papers. His prose brings our cases to life in a way I could never hope to achieve. He's a most talented writer."

Watson cleared his throat. "I say, Holmes, that's kind of you to say so. I try my best."

Knight smiled at the exchange. Then he said, "I've some news that might interest you both. After finding out about Harry, I visited Miss Fairchild to apologise for my involvement in her misfortune, hoping that she might forgive me. She was pleased to say that the money Matthews stole from her had been returned in full. She was quite relieved, as you can imagine."

Holmes nodded approvingly. "Excellent. I trust she's recovering from her ordeal?"

"As well as can be expected," Knight replied. "She's understandably wary now, but I believe the return of her savings has gone a long way towards mending her spirits."

Watson asked, "And what of Mr Thorne? Has there been any development in his situation?"

Knight's face brightened. "Ah, yes. When I learned of Matthews' involvement, I took it upon myself to visit Mr Thorne's former employer. I explained the circumstances surrounding the fabricated story."

"How did they respond?" Holmes asked.

"Quite favourably, actually," Knight said. "The editor was grateful for the clarification. He even suggested running a story about the whole affair."

Watson's eyebrows shot up. "Really? That's quite remarkable."

Knight said, "I agreed to it, but on one condition: that Mr Thorne be reinstated and that he write the piece himself."

Holmes leaned back in his chair, an approving glint in his eye. "A clever stipulation, Mr Knight. And the editor's response to that?"

"He agreed without hesitation," Knight replied. "It seems Mr Thorne's reputation for accuracy and integrity still holds weight, despite the unfortunate incident."

Watson beamed. "That's wonderful news! I'm sure Mr Thorne will be overjoyed to return to his profession. What of Mr Endicott? Did you pay him a visit as well?"

Knight said, "I did. I felt it was important to apologise to him personally for the unfortunate circumstances."

Before Knight could continue, Holmes raised his hand, a glint of intrigue in his eyes. "If I may, might I venture a guess as to Mr Endicott's response?"

"By all means, Mr Holmes. I'd be most interested to hear your deduction."

Holmes steepled his fingers beneath his chin, his gaze focused on some distant point. "I believe Mr Endicott accepted your apology with grace. Moreover, I suspect he saw the potential for a rather entertaining anecdote in the whole affair. One he might share at social gatherings, perhaps?"

Knight's eyes widened in astonishment. "Why, that's exactly what happened! Mr Endicott was quite jovial about the whole thing. But how did you know that he would do that, Mr Holmes?"

"In our brief interaction with Mr Endicott, I was able to form a reasonably accurate assessment of his character," Holmes explained. "Given the circumstances and what I observed of the man, it seemed the most logical outcome."

Knight shook his head in amazement. "Mr Holmes, I'm impressed with your deductive abilities. I must say, this entire experience has given me pause for thought."

"Oh?" Watson prompted.

Knight continued, "I've come to realise the weight of responsibility that comes with my profession. I plan to be more cautious in the future, to emphasise to my clients that the future isn't set in stone, no matter the general guidance I give them. It's crucial they understand that their choices and actions play a significant role in shaping their destinies."

Holmes nodded approvingly. "A wise decision. It's refreshing to see someone in your line of work taking such a thoughtful approach."

With a final expression of gratitude, Knight took his leave.

As the door closed behind their visitor, Watson turned to his friend with a mischievous glint in his eye. "Well, Holmes, since we're on the subject of predictions, would you care to hazard a guess as to what the rest of our day holds?"

"My dear Watson, I predict a most restful afternoon for us both. Perhaps a quiet evening with a good book and a glass of brandy?"

Watson grinned, nodding in agreement. "That sounds positively delightful. And what of tomorrow? Any premonitions about our next case?"

"Ah, tomorrow," Holmes mused. "Who can say what mysteries tomorrow might bring? But of one thing I am certain, my dear friend."

"And what's that?" Watson asked, intrigued.

Holmes leaned back in his chair, a confident smile playing on his face. "Whatever perplexing case may come our way, I have no doubt that together, we shall solve it."

The Sherlock Holmes series

Book 1 – Sherlock Holmes and The Missing Portrait

Book 2 – Sherlock Holmes and The Haunted Museum

Book 3 – Sherlock Holmes and The Hasty Holiday

Book 4 – Sherlock Holmes and The Baker Street Thefts

Book 5 – Sherlock Holmes and The Lamplighter's Mystery

Book 6 – Sherlock Holmes and The Vanishing Act

Book 7 – Sherlock Holmes and The Cat Burglar

Book 8 – Sherlock Holmes and The Unwanted Client

Book 9 – Sherlock Holmes and The Other Detective

Book 10 – Sherlock Holmes and Dr Watson's Disappearance

A note from the author

For as long as I can remember, I have loved reading mystery books. It started with Enid Blyton's Famous Five, and The Secret Seven. As I got older, I progressed to Agatha Christie books, and of course, Sir Arthur Conan Doyle's Sherlock Holmes.

I love the characters of Sherlock Holmes and Dr Watson, and the Victorian era that the stories are set in. It seemed only natural that one day, I would write some of my own Sherlock stories. I love creating new mysteries for Mr Holmes, and his trusty companion, Dr John Watson. It's not just the era itself that seems to ignite ideas within me; it's also the characters who were around at that time, and the lives they led.

This story has been checked for errors, but if you see anything we have missed and you'd like to let us know about them, please email mabel@mabelswift.com

You can hear about my new releases by signing up for my newsletter: www.mabelswift.com As a thank you for subscribing, I will send you a free short story: Sherlock Holmes and The Curious Clock.

If you'd like to contact me, you can get in touch via mabel@mabelswift.com I'd be delighted to hear from you.

Best wishes

Mabel

www.ingramcontent.com/pod-product-compliance
Lightning Source LLC
Chambersburg PA
CBHW051133160726
47997CB00019B/2350